It's Spring!

It's

by Else Holmelund Minarik
pictures by
Margaret Bloy Graham

Spring!

Greenwillow Books, New York

Library of Congress Cataloging-in-Publication Data
Minarik, Else Holmelund.
It's spring! / by Else Holmelund Minarik;
pictures by Margaret Bloy Graham.
p.   cm.
Summary: Pit and Pat celebrate the arrival
of spring by jumping over each other and through
the spring flowers.
ISBN 0-688-07619-X.   ISBN 0-688-07620-3 (lib. bdg.)
[1. Spring—Fiction.]   I. Graham, Margaret Bloy, ill.   II. Title.
PZ7.M652It 1989
[E]—dc19   87-37202   CIP   AC
Watercolor paints were used for the
full-color illustrations.
The text type is ITC Weideman Medium.

For
Becky Sharp-Claws

Pit and Pat were giddy.

"It's spring!" said Pit.
"Spring, spring, spring," said Pat.

"I feel so happy I could
jump over a tulip," said Pit.

"I could jump over a bush," said Pat.

"I could jump over a tree," said Pit.

"I could jump over
a house," said Pat.

"I could jump over
an island," said Pit.

"I could jump over

a mountain," said Pat.

"I could jump over

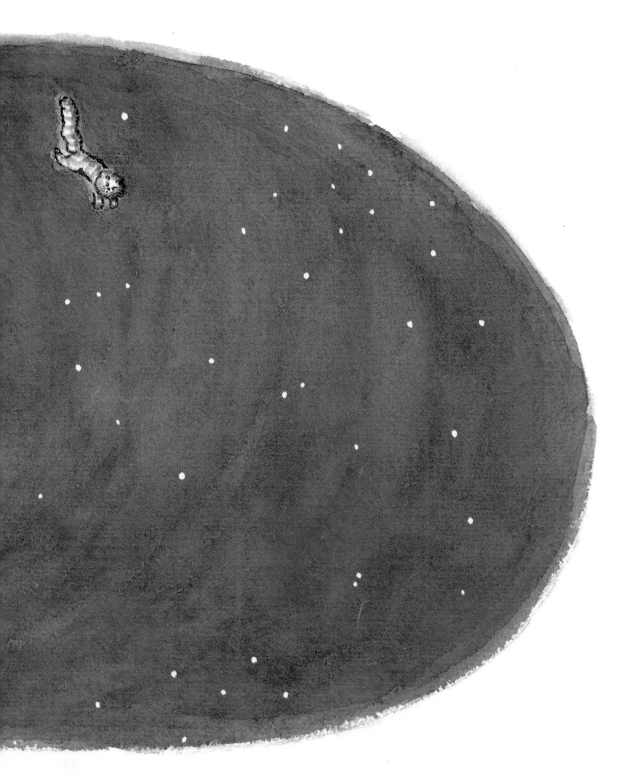

the moon," said Pit.

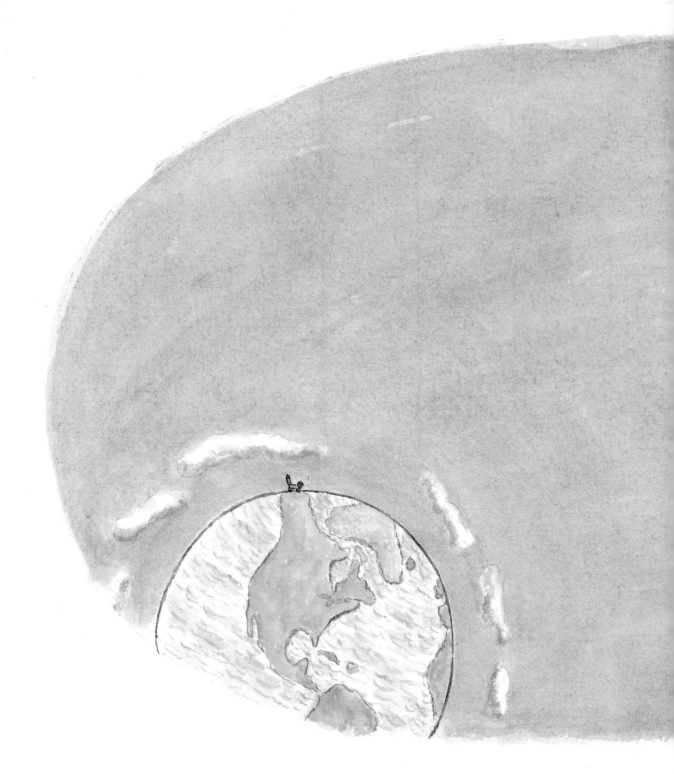

"I could jump over

the sun," said Pat.

"I'll just jump over you,"
said Pit to Pat.

"And then I'll jump over you,"
said Pat to Pit.

So they jumped over each other
all through the tulips

and the daffodils
and the pretty little violets,

because it was spring!